Pet to School Day

by Hilary Robinson

illustrated by Tim Archbold

ZERO TO TEN

This edition published 2010 by Zero to Ten Ltd,
Part of the Evans Publishing Group,
2A Portman Mansions,
Chiltern Street,
London, W1U 6NR

British Library Cataloguing in Publication Data
A CIP catalogue record for this book is available from
the British Library

ISBN: 9781840895841

Printed in China by New Era Printing Co. Ltd

"Today is pet day,"
said Mr Spink.

"Where's your pet, sir?"

"At home. He's too wild."

"Is he a bull?"

"Is he an elephant?"

"No," said Mr Spink.
"My pet is a...

...dinosaur!"

"Have you had him for
thousands of years?"

"I caught him on Sunday.
He wears a red collar, eats
trees and drinks from the bath."

"Where can you catch
dinosaurs?"
"In a dinosaur park."

"How?"
"With a dinosaur net,"
replied Mr Spink.

"Can anyone do that?"

"Only with a permit," said Mr Spink.
"When you catch a dinosaur you get
a badge like mine."

"How can you get a permit?"
asked James.

"You have to show that you are a brave dinosaur warrior," said Mr Spink.

"You're not!"

"How do you know I'm not?"
asked Mr Spink.

"Because you're scared of
spiders and," said James,
"to prove it, this is...

Max!"